£4.99

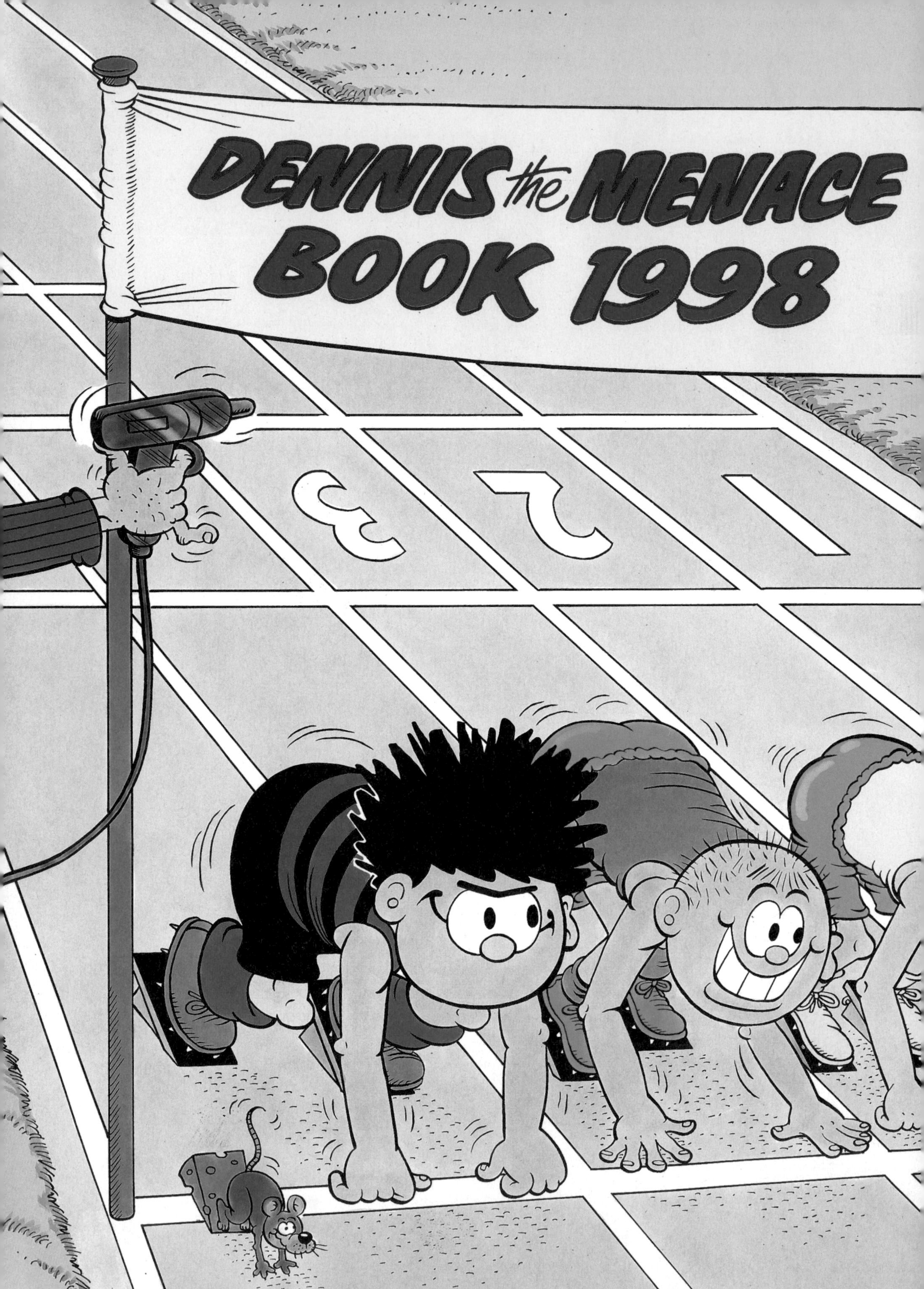

Printed and Published in Great Britain by D. C. Thomson & Co. Ltd., 185 Fleet Street, London EC4A 2HS.
ISBN 0-85116-645-8

START
YOU CAN DO IT, WALTER
WATER
SMELLING SALTS
TRAINEE
PLOOP!
GLUE
SQUASH

name game
ERIK THE NASTY AND "FOE FLATTENER". HIS HAMMER.
PRESS
I MUST GIVE GREAT NAMES LIKE THAT TO MY WEAPONS!
GNESH!
DENNIS'S WEAPON STORE
MUST BOARD UP MY GREENHOUSE!
AND MY WINDOWS!
STRETCH
MEET "WINDOWSHATTERER"!
ARE MY TROUSERS OK?
SNAP!
SNAP!
SO MUCH FOR "WINDOWSHATTERER". WHAT DO YOU CALL IT NOW?
I'LL CALL IT "WALTERWORRIER" NOW!
GNEE! GNEE!
Soon–
OOOER!
MEET "SOFTYSOAKER"!
WEEDS

EH?
IT'S MORE LIKE "FLOWER FRESHENER"!
SUCK!
WINDOW CLEANER
GOOD OLD "GNASHERSPLASHER"!
SPRAAY!
SWOOSH!
Later–
MEET "THUNDERSNAPPER"!
CRACK!
SNAP!
CRACK!
SNAP!
SNAP!
CRACK!
SWISH!
DROP
BITE
BITE
HOI, YOU...
ULP!
SWING
YAHOOOO!
GRAB
SNIP!
EH?
AND SO THE MENACE'S WEAPON, "THUNDERSNAPPER" PROVES NO MATCH FOR DAD AND HIS MIGHTY **"ROSEPRUNER"**!
NAMING WEAPONS? HUH!

SOMETHING SOFT
SOFT-CENTRED CHOCOLATES
SQUEAL!
SQUEEZE!
SQUEEZE!
CHOCS
SOFT MUD
SPLOT!
SPLAT!
SPLUDGE!
BULL'S-EYE!
LEAP!
THUD!
...AND PILLOWS
FLUMFF
GREAT FUN!
FLUP
SOFT DRINKS
DENNIS!
SWOOSH!
SWOOSH!
SHAKE!
SHAKE!
SHAKE!

FOR DENNIS
SOFT WORDS
WHISPER . . . THEN WE'LL . . . WHISPER . . .
SOFT DOVETS . . .
WHEEE!
WHEEE!
A SOFT LANDING!
SOFT TOYS
SOFTIES CHALET
PUSH!
SHOVE!
NGH! TOO HEAVY TO PUSH!
THROW!
SOMETHING HARD FOR WALTER
GOODY! DENNIS LET ME DO THESE HARD SUMS PUNISHMENT EXERCISE!
SAP!
SHARP PENCILS
SPARE PAPER

LOCK, SHOCK and BARROW
At Walter's house—
OH, BOTHER! I'VE FORGOTTEN MY KEY! NOW I WON'T BE ABLE TO HAVE MUMSY'S TEA READY FOR HER WHEN SHE COMES HOME.
HERE'S A CHANCE TO TAKE THE MICKEY OUT OF WALTER!
STAMP!
DON'T WORRY, WALTER—I'LL SHOULDER IT OPEN FOR YOU!
ZOOM!
YEEK!
FAINT
OUCH!
THUD!
ZOOM!
TELL YOU WHAT...
FLOP
... YOU BURST THE DOOR DOWN!
YEEK!
ZOOM!
TRUNDLE
HEY! DO YOU WANT TO GET IN OR NOT?
SCRAMBLE
BUMP
GNASHEE! GNASHEE!

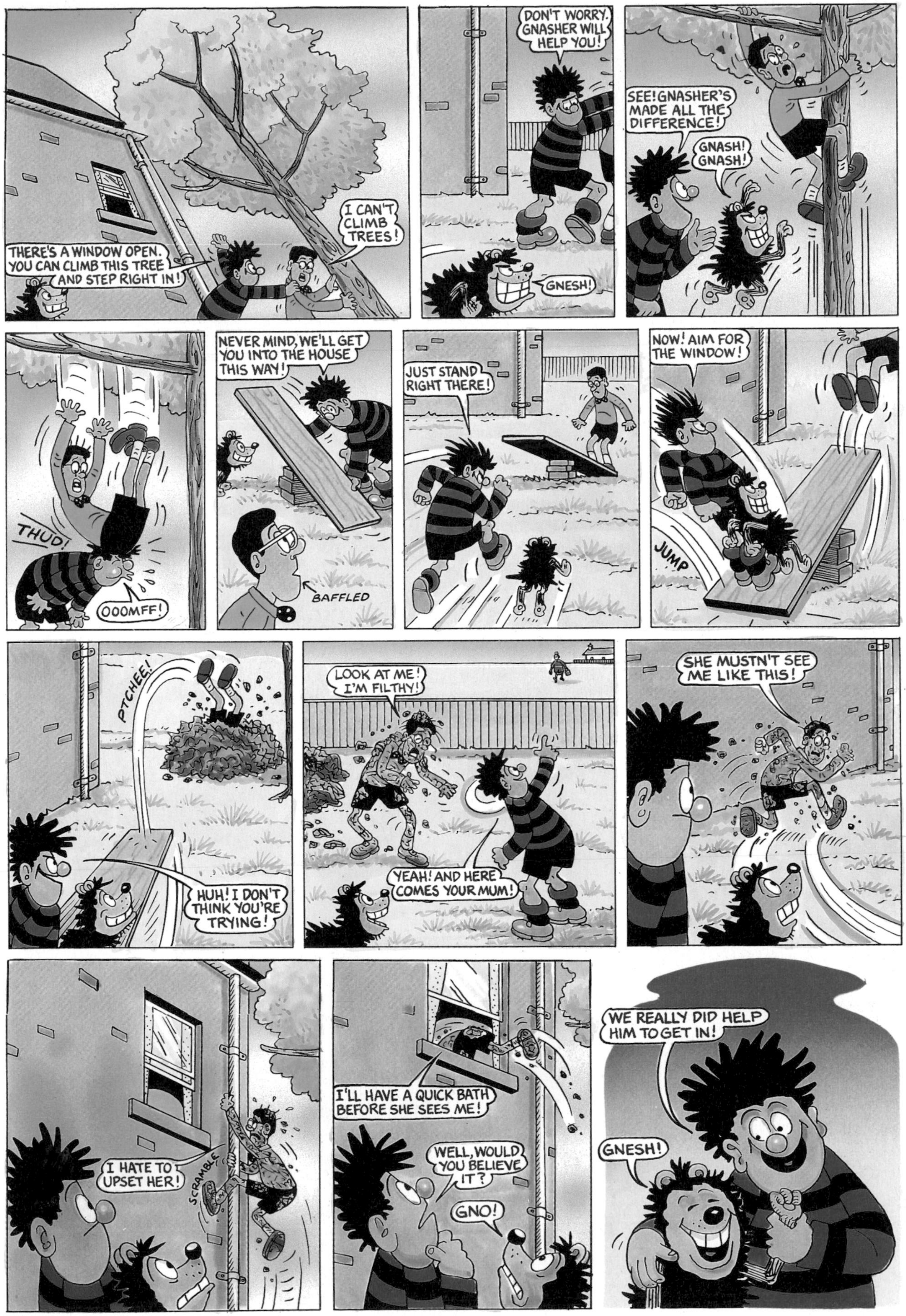

THERE'S A WINDOW OPEN. YOU CAN CLIMB THIS TREE AND STEP RIGHT IN!
I CAN'T CLIMB TREES!
DON'T WORRY. GNASHER WILL HELP YOU!
GNESH!
SEE! GNASHER'S MADE ALL THE DIFFERENCE!
GNASH! GNASH!
THUD!
OOOMFF!
NEVER MIND, WE'LL GET YOU INTO THE HOUSE THIS WAY!
BAFFLED
JUST STAND RIGHT THERE!
NOW! AIM FOR THE WINDOW!
JUMP
PTCHEE!
HUH! I DON'T THINK YOU'RE TRYING!
LOOK AT ME! I'M FILTHY!
YEAH! AND HERE COMES YOUR MUM!
SHE MUSTN'T SEE ME LIKE THIS!
I HATE TO UPSET HER!
SCRAMBLE
I'LL HAVE A QUICK BATH BEFORE SHE SEES ME!
WELL, WOULD YOU BELIEVE IT?
GNO!
WE REALLY DID HELP HIM TO GET IN!
GNESH!

OFF COLOUR MENACE
WHAT A SOPPY COLOUR!
THAT MEANS HE'S THE RACE LEADER!
ZOOM!
12
GREAT IDEA HAVING DIFFERENT COLOURED JERSEYS FOR DIFFERENT THINGS!
KING OF THE MEASLES
3
ZOOM!
Soon—
BRITISH AMERICAN FOOTBALL TEAM
THIS LOT NEED SOME TOUGH OPPOSITION!
YAHOO!
BUMP
ZOOM!
SPLAT!
AFTER THAT BRUISING, I AWARD MYSELF THE...
GRR!
... BLACK AND BLUE JERSEY!
GNAHOO!

SCREAM!
THAT'S WALTER'S VOICE!
SOB! HE'S TRYING TO STING MY NOSE!
BZZZ!
MY UNEXPECTED HERO!
SWISH!
THWACK!
ONLY I GET TO MENACE WALTER'S NOSE!
HEE-HEE!
Soon—
YELLOW JERSEY FOR WASP MENACING!
NO GREENS TODAY, MUM?
SORRY, DAD, I KNOW YOU LIKE THEM!
DAD
WANT GREENS, EH?
ZOOM
BZZZ!
HEY!
DAD
FOR THAT LAWN MENACING— THE GREEN AND BLACK JERSEY!
ZOOM!
COME HERE, YOU!
DAD
PUFF! PUFF!
SPIN
IF YOU AWARD YOURSELF COLOURED JERSEYS, READERS, TAKE THE OLD ONES OFF FIRST!
GRAB
DAD
GASP! WHEEZE!

POLO STINT
LOVELY GAME OF POLO!
SUPAH!
GENTLE TAP
SNOBS! I'D BE GREAT AT THAT GAME!
CAN'T PLAY—YOU DON'T HAVE A PONY!
At home—
I DON'T NEED A PONY...
...I'VE GOT MY TRUSTY STEED!
ZOOM!
WHEELIES
TA!
SNATCH
DANGER MEN AT WORK
ZOOM!
EEK!
SHAKE
TACKS
HERE I AM, SOFTIES!

BAH!
HISS!
HISS!
BURST!
TEE-HEE!
NEVER MIND, ROUGH BOY— I'LL GET YOU A HORSE!
At Walter's house—
CAN'T BELIEVE THIS!
THIS WAY!
NO GOOD TO A MENACE, HUH!
BLUSH
ROCK
TITTER! I AM HAVING FUN TODAY!
WANT TO SHOW ME SOMETHING GNASHER?
GNASH! GNASH! GNASH!
TUG
POINT
OH, YOU CLEVER LITTLE HOUND, YOU!
At polo pitch—
YOURS, OLD CHAPPIE!
CLICK!
RUMBLE!
WH-WHAT WAS THAT?
SWISH!
WAHOO!
WAH!
THWACK!
SHATTER
BELLOW!
CRASH!
WOAH, BOY!
ZOOM!
TEE-HEE! PLAYING WATER POLO, DENNIS?
SPLADOSH!

MENACEFAX
A LOOK INSIDE DENNIS'S PERSONAL ORGANISER.
SHOPPING LIST
Peashooter
Brussels sprouts (for Brussels sprouts shooter)
Cabbage (for cabbage cannon)
Bag of treacle toffees for Gran's birthday. (I've pinched her false teeth so she won't be able to eat it and will probably give me all of it.)
Flour - to make flour bombs and to cover me and Gnasher when we pretend to be snowmen to avoid being caught by the people we've flour-bombed!
One large boot - to kick myself when I realise it's June and snowmen disguises aren't really much good.
FACTFILE ON ENEMIES
WALTER (Prince of Softies)
Frightened of most things. This pathetic specimen is even scared of butterflies - he's worried that their fluttering might blow him over. An energetic ballet dancer, particularly when he has a bowl of ice-cubes down his tights.
BERTIE BLENKINSOP
Not quite Prince of Softies but he did come second in the Beanotown Rosebud Princess contest. Loves cooking and knitting and once knitted bootees and a frilly bonnet for his baby carrots.
SPOTTY PERKINS
Pimply pal of Walter and Bertie. Has been known to cover himself in so much spot ointment that his teddy shot up in the air when he gave it it's hourly hug.

NOTES
I hid Gnasher's bone in the teapot-
Dad doesn't know why his tea
tasted funny!
Gnasher hates the smell
of cat food. The postman's
taken to brushing cat
food on his uniform
to keep Gnasher at bay.
Mind you, now he is being mobbed
by tom cats!
Walter has given me some
lovely over-ripe tomatoes.
Seems the ones I've been
pelting him with have been
too hard for the weedy
sap!
AUTOGRAPHS
Curly
Pie-face
sorry for
the gravy stain-
pie being eaten
at the time.
gnipper
Gnasher
BILLY WHIZZ
Sir Les Pretend O.B.E.
Danny (from Bash St.)
Uffins
MENACE GOLD AWARD TESTS
MAKING STINKBOMBS
EGG THROWING
NEIGHBOUR ANNOYING
ANT TRAINING
CATAPULTING
INK PELLET FIRING
NIPPING SOFTIES (with crab claws)
GNASHING (applies only to canine members)

PLAY IT AGAIN, SAP!

EEK!
HE LIKES A DANCE, TOO!
PLINK!
PLONK!
I RECKON GNASHER'S PIANO PLAYING WAS BETTER THAN YOURS! LET'S SEE IF I CAN HELP YOUR STYLE ANY!
EH?
HMM! NOT MUCH OF AN IMPROVEMENT.
GNICE!
TUG!
PLINK!
PLANK!
PLONK!
MAYBE YOUR FEET ARE MORE TALENTED THAN YOUR HANDS!
TUG
NOW, THAT'S MUCH BETTER!
SO!
HOWL!
OOPS!
THAT WILL BE ENOUGH FOR TODAY, WALTER. YOU CAN GO!
SUPPOSE WE'D BETTER, TOO!
GNESH!
OH, NO, YOU DON'T! AS YOU SEEM TO LIKE MUSIC SO MUCH, YOU CAN STAY AND LISTEN TO MY NEXT PUPIL!
HEH-HEH!
GNURK!
GLURK!
AND HERE SHE COMES NOW!
EH? HER?
UNLOCK THE DOOR! OPEN THE WINDOW! AT LEAST LEND US YOUR EAR-PLUGS! NO WONDER SHE'S CALLED IVY THE TERRIBLE!
TERRIBLE DIN!
EAR-PLUGS

GIVE US A BREAK
DAD'S CAR'S CONKED OUT AGAIN!
GRIND!
GNERK!
DAD 1
CAN'T BE REPAIRED ANY MORE, SIR. IT'LL HAVE TO GO TO THE BREAKER'S YARD FOR SCRAP!
SOB! SOB!
COUGH! COUGH!
BREAKER'S YARD
VROOM!
HMMM...
DAD 1
HAVING TROUBLE, MISTER?
THIS TOUGH OLD CAR WON'T COME APART!
DAD'S CAR
GNASH!
GNASH!
GNASH!
'BYE, AND THANKS!
BREAKER'S YARD
GNASH! CHOMP!
CHUCKLE! THE MAN SAYS YOU CAN HAVE A JOB THERE ANYTIME, GNASHER.
SLOO!
REWARD

HEH-HEH! WE HAVE OUR OWN BREAKER'S YARD!
BRING YOUR OLD PEDAL CARS AND CARTIES HERE
MY FLYING DISC'S BROKEN, DENNIS!
OK. I'LL SOON FIND SOMETHING FOR YOU!
TRY THESE HUB CAPS!
PTCHEEE!
OOPS! MISSED!
ER—A BIT WILD, EH?
CRASH!
TINKLE!
CHOP
Later—
WHAT IS IT, PIEFACE?
I'VE NO HOOPS FOR MY HOOPLA!
HOW'S THIS FOR A HOOPLA SET?
PLOP
GREAT!
MISSED!
WAH! MY CAKES!
PLOP!
OINKEE! CHOMP!
HM... I KNOW HOW TO BREAK UP THESE THINGS.
GNESH!
ROLL UP! ONLY 10p FOR THE DODGEMS!
BUMP
CRASH!
BUMP!
THIS LOOKS SUPER FUN!
I'LL TAKE THIS!
OOPS! WE WERE RICH, GNASHER!
IT'LL PAY FOR SOME OF THE DAMAGE YOU'VE DONE—ALONG WITH YOUR NEXT MONTH'S POCKET-MONEY!
HA-HA! THE BREAKER IS BROKE NOW!
BAH!
TUG

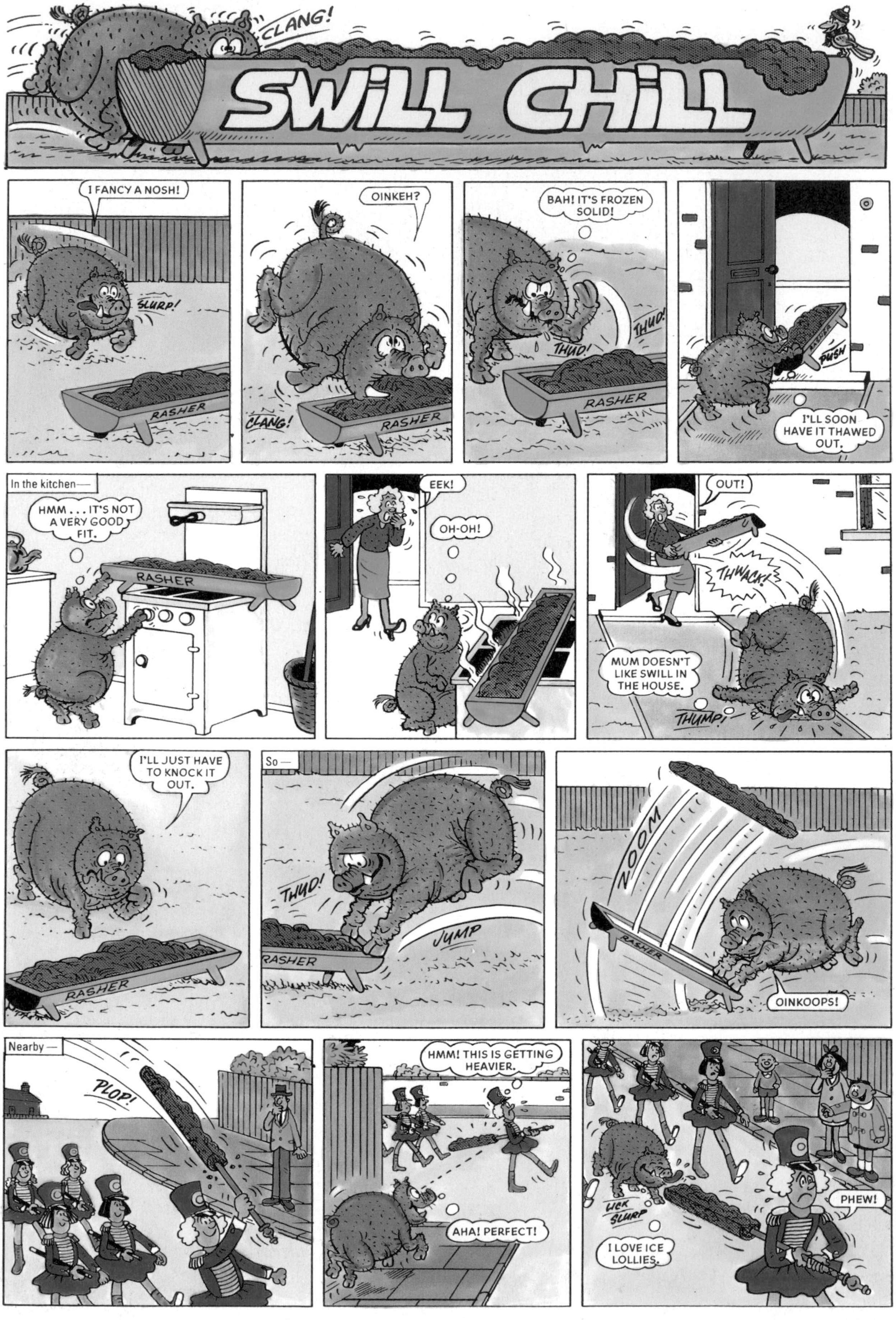
CLANG!
SWILL CHILL
I FANCY A NOSH!
SLURP!
RASHER
OINKEH?
CLANG!
RASHER
BAH! IT'S FROZEN SOLID!
THUD!
THUD!
RASHER
PUSH
I'LL SOON HAVE IT THAWED OUT.
In the kitchen—
HMM . . . IT'S NOT A VERY GOOD FIT.
RASHER
EEK!
OH-OH!
OUT!
THWACK!
MUM DOESN'T LIKE SWILL IN THE HOUSE.
THUMP!
I'LL JUST HAVE TO KNOCK IT OUT.
RASHER
So—
THUD!
JUMP
RASHER
ZOOM
RASHER
OINKOOPS!
Nearby—
PLOP!
HMM! THIS IS GETTING HEAVIER.
AHA! PERFECT!
LICK SLURP
I LOVE ICE LOLLIES.
PHEW!

DENNIS' WEATHER REPORT
THERE'S A TORNADO COMING!
BALLET CLASS
GOTCHA, WALTER!
EEK!
GRAB!
WHOOSH!
SHRIEK!
WANT TO GO FOR A SPIN?
YIKES!

ATTEN-SHUN!
FOR THE COLONEL'S BATTLE ROLL OF HONOUR
18:15
TOILET
The Battle of Waterloo
WATERLOO STATION, THAT IS!
The Battle of Stamford Bridge
BLOOMIN' DECK CHAIR!
HASTINGS BEACH
The Battle of Hastings

TRAFALGAR SQUARE
BOOM!
BOOM!
The Battle of Trafalgar
HAVE AT YE!
VARLET!
GARDEN CENTRE
The Wars of the Roses
I SAW THIS PLANT FIRST!
Brian Walker
LET'S CALL IT A DRAW!
I AGREE!
The Hundred Years War
WAAAGH!
The Battle of Bannockburn
SPLAT!

GET YOUR SKATES ON!
ICE RINK
WHAT'S WRONG? WE HAVEN'T MENACED YOU YET!
BOO-HOO!
MY ICESKATING PARTNER LEFT ME FOR THAT ICE HOCKEY PLAYING RUFFIAN!
CAN'T SAY I BLAME HER!
GNO!
WAIL!
OK, OK—GNASHER AND I'LL GET YOU ANOTHER PARTNER.
GNESH!
FASHION SHOP
BACK DOOR
THIS DUMMY WILL DO!
MEET AMELIA, WALTER—SHE, ER—DOESN'T TALK MUCH!
SHOVE
AS LONG AS SHE'S A GOOD SKATER!
YOU DANCE DIVINELY, AMELIA!
SNIGGER!
SCREAM!
HAR! HAR!
CLUNK!
GNASHEE!

I'LL BE S-SENT TO JAIL! HELP ME!
HEH! HEH! IT'S ONLY A DUMMY!
PLOP!
At the ice rink cafe—
WE'LL NEED ANOTHER PARTNER FOR YOU!
TEA
MENU
Outside—
YOU'RE KEEN ON SPORT, TESSA...
So—
TIME TO LIFT HER, WALTER!
Then—
WHERE'S WALTER?
OH, THERE HE IS!
I'M NOT SKATING WITHOUT A PARTNER!
MUMFLE!
So—
CHATTER! CHATTER!
GNASHER WILL HAVE TO BE YOUR PARTNER!
HE'LL LOOK RIDICULOUS IN A SKATING SKIRT!
NO, HE WON'T — YOU'LL BE WEARING IT!
SHAKE
SHAKE
At the skating contest—
GLIDE
GLIDE
6 0 6 0 6 0
JUST AS WELL!
WE'VE WON! WONDERFUL!
I MUST GIVE MY PARTNER A KISS!
GNASH! DON'T YOU DARE!
POUT
HEH! HEH! GNASHER'S MY PARTNER, WALTER—DON'T FORGET IT!

SNOW JOKE
WAHOO! SNOW!
GNASHEE!
BLOW
COME ON—WE'RE GOING TO THE PLAY PARK!
DRAG
GNAY GNARK?
SO—
SHOVE
ZOOM!
WHIRR!
GRAB
SLIDE—E
YAHOO! CAN'T DO THIS IN SUMMER!
I'M DRAWING A SNOWFLAKE!
WALTER, FUTURE KING OF THE SOFTIES.
GRAB
LET ME GO!
HAR! HAR!
GNOKAY!
ZOOM!
WHUMP!

SHAKE
RUB
TH-THAT W-WAS C-COLD!
SOME MORE PLAY PARK MENACING!
PLOP!
RUMBLE!
ERK!
MISSED ME!
ZOOM!
PUSH
WH-WHAT'S TH-THAT SHADOW?
TOPPLE
OH, NO!
HEH-HEH! THERE'S NO ESCAPE!
FLUMFF!
Later—
OH, GNASHER! THERE'S A CAT HERE FOR YOU TO CHASE!
PTCHEEE!
STAMP
GNASHEE! A CAT? GRRREATT!
HEH! HEH! A SNOW-CAT, THAT IS!
ULP! THAT KIND OF "CAT"— RUN LIKE FUN, GNASHER!
SCREECH OF PAWS
PURR!
PURRR!
SNOW-CAT
DAD BORROWED THIS FROM THE PARK RANGER.

WRAP UP!
I'M OFF, MUMSIE!
I HOPE YOU'RE WELL WRAPPED UP!
WALTER, KING OF THE SOFT FRONTIER
HANG ON, WALTER! MUSTN'T HAVE MUMSIE WORRYING!
SNATCH
WE'LL WRAP YOU UP, SOFTY!
FLOP!
STOP GETTING DENNIS TO DO YOUR DIRTY WORK, WALTER. I KNOW YOU'VE ALWAYS FANCIED MY BONNET!
SNATCH
STAMP
THESE BANDAGES WILL KEEP YOU WARM!
THROB
THIS IS REALLY WRAPPING YOU UP, WALTER!
DENNIS!
HOW DARE YOU RAID THE FIRST-AID CABINET!
TUG
TUG

HAVEN'T BEEN VERY SUCCESSFUL SO FAR, WALTER, BUT I KNOW SOMETHING THAT'LL KEEP YOU SWELTERING!
GNASHER'S KENNEL! HE'S ALWAYS VERY COSY IN IT!
OOOH!
GNASHER
OOGH! IT'S HORRID! DISGUSTING! TAKE IT OFF!
NONSENSE!
EEK!
A BIT UNTIDY PERHAPS, BUT NOT DISGUSTING!
HMM! HOW ELSE CAN WE WRAP YOU UP TO STOP MUMSIE WORRYING?
GOT IT!
HELP! STOP IT! LEAVE ME!
YOU'RE WELL WRAPPED UP. WE COULD POST YOU OFF TO SPAIN AND YOU'D BE VERY COSY!
UNWRAP ME!
Then—
YEEK!
WOBBLE
TRIP
LADIES CIRCLE FANCY DRESS CONTEST TODAY
A PARCEL! DEFINITELY THE MOST ORIGINAL! HE WINS FIRST PRIZE!
WOBBLE
UGH! WE'VE HELPED HIM WIN A CONTEST!
HAR! HAR! BUT HE'S WELCOME TO THE PRIZE!
FANCY DRESS CONTEST TODAY
MUMSIE WILL BE PLEASED! THIS WILL KEEP ME SO WARM!
SOFTEST JERSEY IN THE WORLD
1ST PRIZE
GNASHEE! GNASHEE!

WALKIES on the WILD SIDE
I REMEMBER ONE COLD WINTER'S AFTERNOON . . .
LOVELY GLOW
NOTHING LIKE SNOOZING IN FRONT OF THE FIRE ON A COLD DAY.
But —
CLICK!
GNASHER WANTS A WALK, MY DEAR.
DRAG
GNO I DON'T!
GOOD EXCUSE FOR ME TO COME TO THE FOOTBALL, THIS.
DRAG
GRRR!
ERK!
ZOOM
I'LL TEACH DAD A LESSON.
WAH!
ZIP
GNASHEE!
EEK!
ZOOM
BUMP!
WOO!
BUMP!
BUMP!
NO . . . NO!
DRAG
ZOOM
DUCK POND
SCREECH TO HALT
SPLOOSH!
THAT WASN'T SUCH A GOOD IDEA!
WARM GLOW
NOW I CAN'T GET NEAR THE FIRE MYSELF.

SHOCKING
ALL OVER THE WORLD!
Curly.
TWANG
PLINK
Pie-face.
BOOM -DA- BOOM
WE'RE THE DINMAKERS! YEAH! YEAH! YEAH!

YOU'RE THE DINMAKERS! NO-NO-NO!
COVER
COVER
COVER
ZIP!
COVER
Z-Z-Z-Z-ZIP!
AW!
PEOPLE HAVE BEEN COMPLAINING ABOUT THE NOISE YOU MAKE!
WHO, DAD?
COVER
SNIGGER!
EH?
NO CHANCE, MY LAD!
CLAMP
CLAMP
CLICK!
CLAMP
OH, NO!
THERE'S TO BE NO MORE PLAYING AROUND HERE EVER AGAIN, DENNIS!
WHAT?!?
WAG!
Sergeant Slipper.
Look at their snaps!
WE'RE GOING ON OUR "SHOCKING ALL OVER THE WORLD" TOUR!
HOORAY!
PEACE AT LAST!

HIM FOR A START!
GULP!
BEANOTOWN CEMETRY
QUIET!
RIP
EEP THE ISE DOWN!
WE WERE PRACTISING FOR A CONCERT TONIGHT!
WAVE
COME ON, DINMAKERS — GIVE ME A SMILE!
WHY, DENNIS?
BECAUSE I'M TAKING PASSPORT PHOTOGRAPHS OF YOU!
COOL!
CLICK
SNAP
CLICK
SNAP
CLICK
GNCOOL!
YOU CAN HAVE YOUR INSTRUMENTS BACK IN THAT CASE!
CLICK
CUDDLE
So—
HEY, WORLD, NOW YOU GOT THE CHANCE . . .
'BYE MENACES
TO FRANCE
LE PUFF PUFF

. . . WE'RE OFF AND ROCKIN', SO LOOK OUT, FRANCE!
BONJOUR!
AARGH! LES DINMAKERS!
QUICK! GET WORKING!
EXTRA SECTION 1
EXTRA SECTION 2
EXTRA SECTION 3
EXTRA SECTION 4
GERMANY
BORDER
FRANCE
HURRY! HURRY!
NEARLY THERE!
Until —
EXTRA SECTION 1578
GASP!
PHEW! MADE IT!
EH?
WELCOME TO GERMANY
LE PUFF PUFF
GERMANY? WHAT HAPPENED TO FRANCE?

RUM-TUM-TIDDLE-TUM TUM-TIDDLE-TUM, TUM-TIDDLE-TIDDLE-TUM-
TAP! TAP!
SLAP!
SLAP!
CLAP! CLAP!
HEY! THAT LOOKS FUN! LET'S TRY IT!
TWANG-TWANG-TWANGLE-TWANG! TWANG-TWANGLE-TWANG! TWANGLE-TWANG-TWANGLE!
BOOM
YEOWL! MY POOR KNEES!
SLAP!
SLAP
SLAP
GNEE-HEE!
SLAP
SLAP
WHEEE
SLAP

HOW DARE YOU SLAP POOR BORIS' KNEES SO MUCH!
THROB! THROB!
ERK! LET'S GO, DINMAKERS!
DER SAUSAGE FACTORY
QUICK! INTO THIS BASKET!
DER SAUSAGE BASKET
SAUSAGE FILLING ON ⟷ OFF
TURN
THIS SAUSAGE SKIN GIVES ME AN IDEA!
TUG!
IF WE TIE THE ROPES TO THE SAUSAGE SKINS . . .
DER SAUSAGE BASKET
TIE
. . . LIKE THIS, WE HAVE OUR VERY OWN . . .
INFLATE
DER SAUSAGE BASKET
. . . HOT AIR BALLOON! YAHOO! WE'RE OFF ON OU
WORLD TOUR AGAIN!
RISE

AH! LOST THEM!
BUMP!
HEH!
DER SAUSAGE BASKET
Inside the factory —
OH, NO! GNASHER'S GOT THE SCENT OF SPICY SAUSAGES!
BLOOP BLOOP
SPICY SAUSAGE NIFF!
CHOMP! DELICIOUS!
LEAP
VILE BREATH
. . . AND USE GNASHER'S HOT, SPICY BREATH . . .
VILE HOT SPICY BREATH
DER SAUSA BASK
Soon —
LET'S PLAY A CONCERT IN THE AIR ABOVE SWITZERLAND!
HEY, YOU SWISS, WON'T YOU LISTEN TO THIS! GONNA PLAY THE KIND A MUSIC THAT YOU JUST CAN'T MISS!
SWISS BORDER
CHEESE
CHEESE
RUMBLE
RUMBLE

Suddenly —
PLINK! PLONK!
TWANG!
SWOOSH!
SWOOSH!
RUMBLE!
I'M STUCK!
SWISS CHEESE
WE'VE GOT TO GET RID OF THEM!
OOH!
MOO!
So —
THIS SHOULD DO IT!
ERK! WE'RE HEADING BACK THE WAY WE CAME!
BLAST OF AIR!
PARP
PARP
BLAST!
PARP
BLAST OF AIR!
BLOW!
BLOW
BLOW

But —
OOPS! WE'RE FLYING PAST BRITAIN!
ZOOM
IRELAND
BRITAIN
On board a nearby plane —
SOUNDS LIKE THUNDER!
BOOM! BOOM!
BOOM-DA-BOOM!
NO! IT'S GNASHER PLAYING HIS DRUMS!
Eventually —
COO! AMERICA!

YIKES! WE'VE BEEN BURST BY THE STATUE OF LIBERTY!
DRIFT
BANG!
BURST
FISSSSSSSSSS
WAAAH!
LOOK! A HUGE CROWD! THEY MUST HAVE KNOWN WE WERE COMING!
BASEBALL STADIUM
WE'RE THE DINMAKERS! YEAH! YEAH! YEAH!
TWANG
BOOM
PLONK
HEY! QUIT THE NOISE! WE GOT A BASEBALL MATCH TO PLAY HERE!
BASEBALL STADIUM
COACH
BOOM-DA
BOOM

SORRY, BUT I CAN'T HEAR YOU FOR ALL THE NOISE WE'RE MAKING!
SWISH
SPIN
SWISH
RIGHT, PITCHERS, LET 'EM HAVE IT!
COACH
THROW
THROW
THROW
RIGHT, DINMAKERS, LET THEM HAVE IT!
SWISH
SWISH
SWISH
WHEE!
WHEE!
WHEE!
WHEE!
COACH
THWACK!
WAAH!
THWACK!
EEK!
THWACK!
AARGH!
THWACK!

GREATEST HOME RUNS WE'VE EVER SEEN!
AMAZING!
BOW!
BOW! BOW!
BOW!
BOW!
CLAP! CLAP!
NEVER MIND A HOM RUN — WHAT ABOU RUN HOME?
On board —
WE'LL ENTERTAIN THE PASSENGERS!
WE'RE PLAYIN' IT LOUD OUT HERE ON THE OCEAN, GOTTA GET THIS SHIP A REAL ROCKIN' MOTION!
CRASH
SHATTER
SHATTER
TINKLE
WE'LL PLAY HERE INSTEAD!
STOMP
PLINK
OI! STOP THAT DIN!
EH?
WHO SAID THAT?

HMMM!
COACH
AFTER THAT DISPLAY, YOU'LL GO HOME IN STYLE, GUYS!
COACH
And—
Queen Elizabeth 2
COACH
CAN'T TAKE ANY MORE OF THIS! GROOGH!
UHH! I'M SEASICK!
PUFF!
PUFF! PANT!
YOU'VE BEEN BANNED FROM THIS SHIP, WE'RE PUTTING YOU ON A DESERT ISLAND!
LOWER
SPLUTCH
THROW
CAN'T A WHALE HAVE A SNOOZE IN PEACE?
EEK!
GNWAAH!
HELP!

W-O-W-!
BLOW
BLOW
I'VE HAD ENOUGH OF YOU LOT!
OOYAH!
WHUMP!
TO BRITAIN
WAAAAAH!
WHEEE
LOOK! IT'S THE DINMAKERS AGAIN!
HA! HA! KEEP GOING, YOU LOT!
Queen Elizabeth 2
Back in Beanotown —
OH, NO! THEY'RE BACK!
LOOKS LIKE OUR PEACE IS OVER!
WHEE
SMASH!
CRASH!
BUMP!
S/P/L/A/T
T/H/U/D

But—
WE WON'T BE ABLE TO PLAY!
SOB! WE LANDED ON OUR GEAR!
GROAN! THEY'RE ALL SMASHED UP!
YES!
YAHOO!
OH-HO!
HUMPH!
GNUMPH!
But—
OH, NO! WE CAN'T HAVE THIS, MEN!
AGREED!
WE'LL GET YOU NEW INSTRUMENTS, DINMAKERS!
EH? WHY ARE THESE BUSINESSMEN DOING THAT?
A. TWANG
MUSICAL INSTRUMENTS
GUITARS
DRUM KITS

And, so —
TWANG
PLINK!
PLONK!
BOOM-DA-BOOM!
CRASH
SHATTER
TINKLE
CRASH
BAH! MY WINDOWS ARE BROKEN!
MY POOR EARS!
GET YOUR EARMUFFS WHILE STOCKS LAST!
GRR! MENACES!
EAR MUFFS
EAR MUFFS KEEPS ALL NOISES OUT
A.PAYNE Glazier
I'M GOING TO PELT THEM WITH FRUIT!
RUB! RUB!
HA! HA!
LOTS OF WORK FOR ME REPAIRING WINDOWS!
B.TURNIP FRESH FRUIT
TOSS!
FRESH FRUIT! BUY YOUR FRESH FRUIT TO THROW AT THE DINMAKERS HERE!
HA-HA! THE DINMAKERS KEEP THESE MEN IN BUSINESS.
ACHE!
THROB!

WHAT DO YOU THINK OF IT SO FAR?
WELL, WE'RE ABOUT HALFWAY THROUGH THE BOOK AND LET'S JUST PAUSE NOW TO HEAR A FEW WORDS FROM THOSE THAT HAVE FEATURED SO FAR!
BUDDA- BUDDA- BUDDA! THEY'RE COMING FROM ALL DIRECTIONS! BANDITS AT TEN O'CLOCK! HALF PAST FOUR TOO IF I'M NOT MISTAKEN! HUNDREDS OF BLIGHTERS. TAKE COVER— I'M GOING IN! WISH ME LUCK, OLD BOY!
MY HAIR HAS LOOKED QUITE NICE SO FAR AND I HOPE MY CLOTHES DON'T MAKE LOOK TOO FAT! I'LL MAKE YOU A NICE CUP OF TEA THEN YOU CAN CARRY ON WITH THE SECOND HALF OF THE BOOK!
GROAN! POCKET MONEY HAS BEEN STOPPED UNTIL GOODNESS KNOWS WHEN! GROUNDED FOR ANOTHER FEW WEEKS AND THAT'S JUST ME! DENNIS ON THE OTHER HAND IS HAVING A BALL- AND HE'LL PROBABLY PUT **THAT** THROUGH SOMEONE'S GREENHOUSE! GROAN!
THERE HAS BEEN A COMPLETE LACK OF FLOWER ARRANGING AND CROCHET TIPS AND PRETTY PICTURES OF PONIES! I WANT TO SEE LOVELY SOFT BUNNIES AND LAMBKINS AND A LOT LESS OF THAT NASTY, RUDE BOY—DENNIS! GLUB! I'M GOING TO TELL MY MUMSIE ON YOU, DENNIS! YOU KNOW I DON'T LIKE TOMATOES IN MY HAIR! BOO-HOO!
GNESH-GNISHTY-GNASTY-GNHEM! GNOSH-GNAARGH-GNIP-GNOH! (Translation) GNESH-GNISHTY-GNASHTY-ER-SORRY, BUT GNASHER IS CURRENTLY CHASING THE POOR TRANSLATOR DOWN DOWN THE ROAD AND I DON'T THINK SHE'S COMING BACK.
HAR-HAR! WHAT A LAUGH! I'M MENACING EVERYONE WITH NO LITTLE HELP FROM GNASHER. I HAVEN'T HAD THIS MUCH FUN SINCE I PUT A QUEEN BEE IN DAD'S BOXER SHORTS AND THE REST OF THE HIVE CAME LOOKING FOR HER. IF THE SECOND HALF'S HALF AS GOOD AS THE FIRST HALF IT'LL BE....ER....UM QUARTER AS GOOD AS THE WHOLE BOOK (BUT MAYBE NOT, 'COS I'M HOPELESS AT MATHS!)

VIDEO NASTY!
ALL THE GROUPS MAKE POP VIDEOS THESE DAYS.
READY TO MAKE OUR POP VIDEO?
DENNIS'S GROUP, THE DINMAKERS
ONE PROBLEM, DENNIS...
...WE DON'T HAVE A CAMERA!
MMM...YES, THAT IS A PROBLEM!
STORE DE POSH
THERE'S ONE IN HERE, LADS!
THIS SHOP IS PROTECTED BY TV.
ARGH!
TV SECURITY
TV
BOOM DA BOOM!

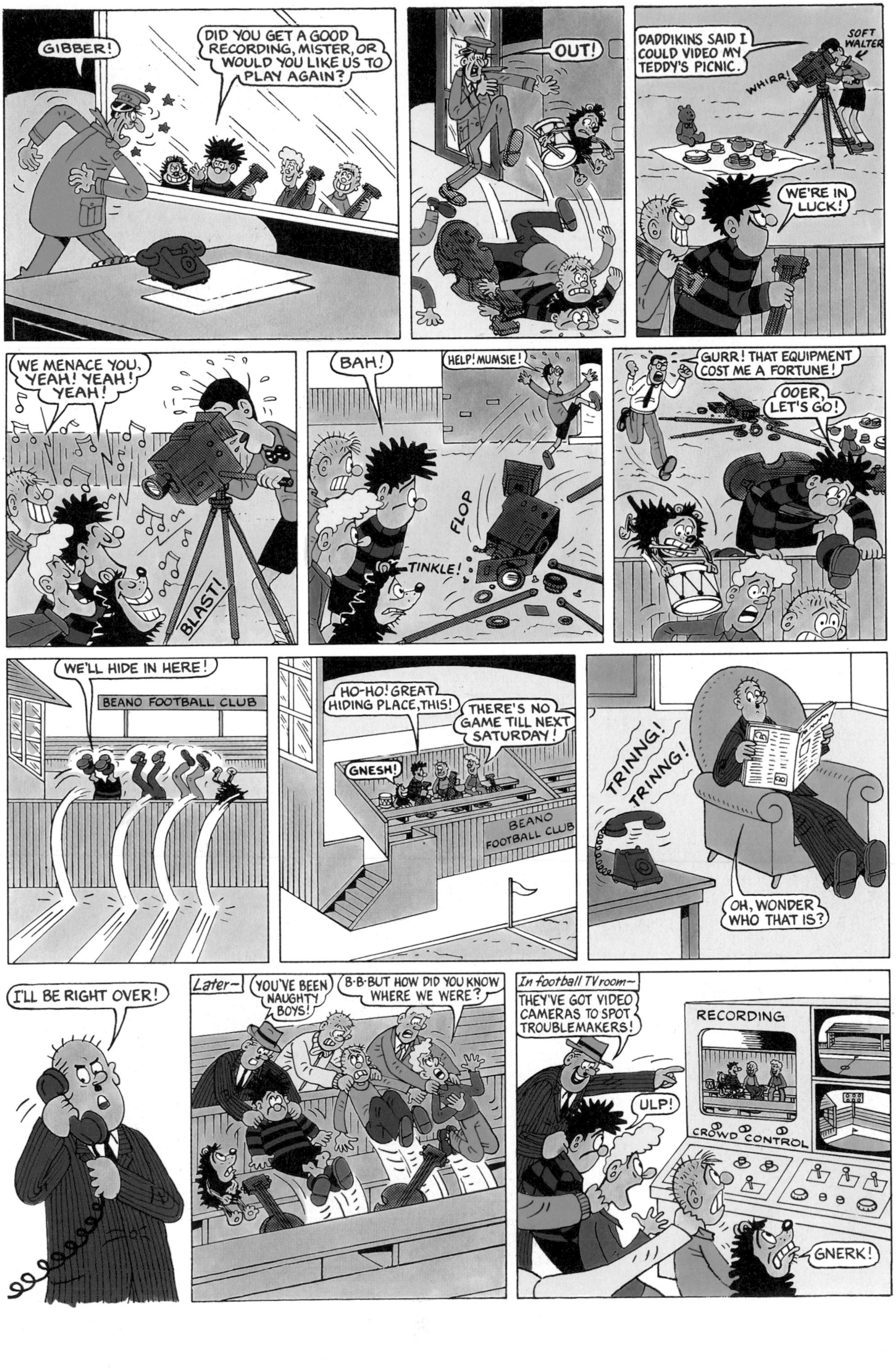
GIBBER!
DID YOU GET A GOOD RECORDING, MISTER, OR WOULD YOU LIKE US TO PLAY AGAIN?
OUT!
DADDIKINS SAID I COULD VIDEO MY TEDDY'S PICNIC.
SOFT WALTER
WHIRR!
WE'RE IN LUCK!
WE MENACE YOU, YEAH! YEAH! YEAH!
BLAST!
BAH!
HELP! MUMSIE!
FLOP
TINKLE!
GURR! THAT EQUIPMENT COST ME A FORTUNE!
OOER, LET'S GO!
WE'LL HIDE IN HERE!
BEANO FOOTBALL CLUB
HO-HO! GREAT HIDING PLACE, THIS!
THERE'S NO GAME TILL NEXT SATURDAY!
GNESH!
BEANO FOOTBALL CLUB
TRINNG!
TRINNG!
OH, WONDER WHO THAT IS?
I'LL BE RIGHT OVER!
Later—
YOU'VE BEEN NAUGHTY BOYS!
B-B-BUT HOW DID YOU KNOW WHERE WE WERE?
In football TV room—
THEY'VE GOT VIDEO CAMERAS TO SPOT TROUBLEMAKERS!
RECORDING
ULP!
CROWD CONTROL
GNERK!

WATCH THE BIRDIE!
IT'S AWFUL! TERRIBLE!
I WOULDN'T SAY THAT, WALTER! IT LOOKS QUITE A NICE BIRDCAGE!
I DIDN'T MEAN THAT. I'VE LOST MY PET BUDGIE!
AW, SHAME!
DOESN'T REALLY MEAN IT
AWSH!
NEVER MIND, WALTER...
Soon—
I'LL BE YOUR PRETEND BUDGIE FOR A WHILE. MAYBE THAT'LL TAKE YOUR MIND OFF LOSING YOUR REAL ONE!
FLAP
FLAP
HOP
HOP
WHAT SORT OF THINGS DID YOUR BUDGIE DO? I BET HE SANG SWEETLY TO YOU!
FLAP
ZOOM
FLAP
HOP
HOP
ZOOM
TWEET! TWEET! CHIRP! TWEET!
FLAP
GNEE-HEE!
EEEK!

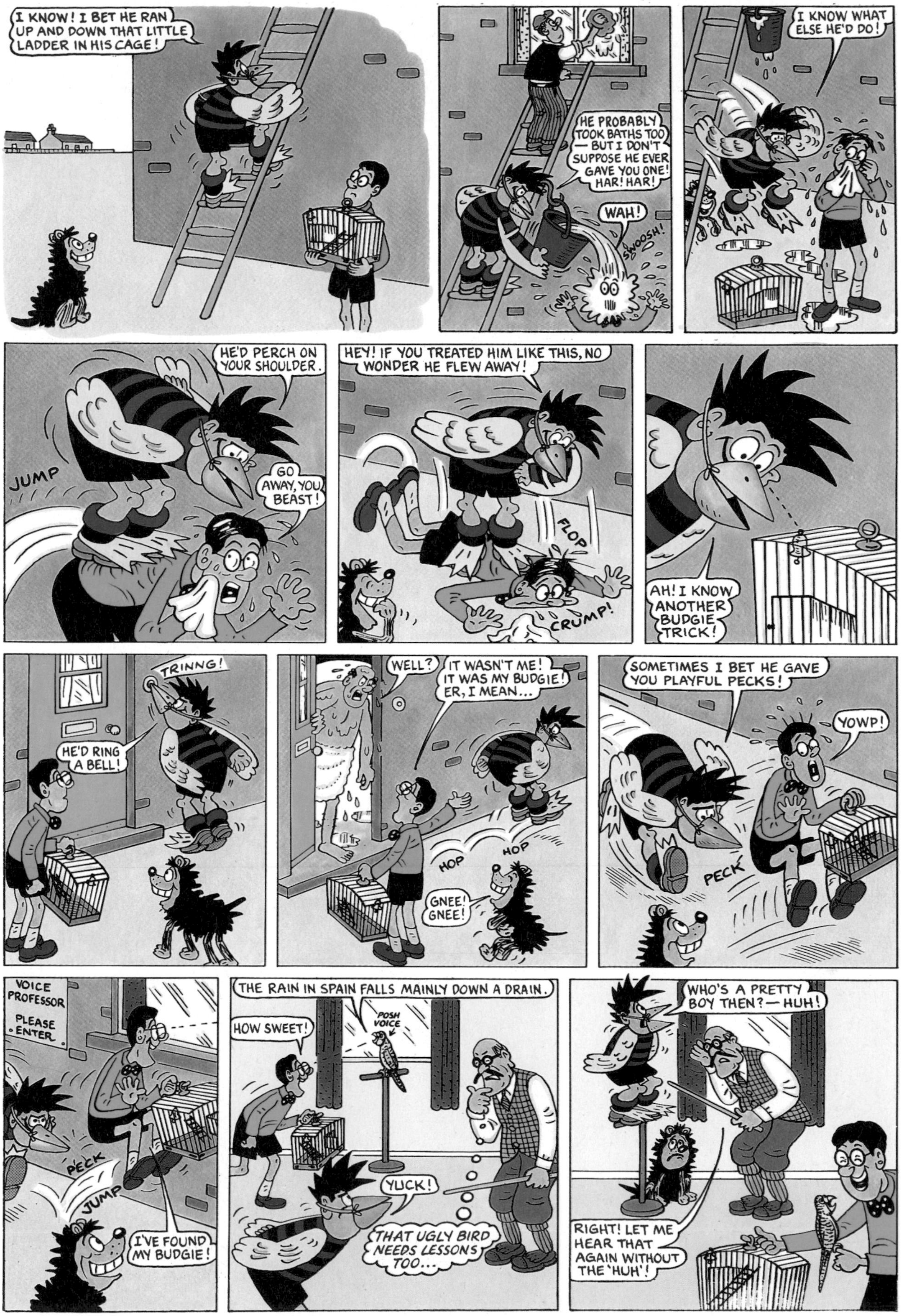

I KNOW! I BET HE RAN UP AND DOWN THAT LITTLE LADDER IN HIS CAGE!
HE PROBABLY TOOK BATHS TOO — BUT I DON'T SUPPOSE HE EVER GAVE YOU ONE! HAR! HAR!
WAH!
SWOOSH!
I KNOW WHAT ELSE HE'D DO!
HE'D PERCH ON YOUR SHOULDER.
JUMP
GO AWAY, YOU BEAST!
HEY! IF YOU TREATED HIM LIKE THIS, NO WONDER HE FLEW AWAY!
FLOP
CRUMP!
AH! I KNOW ANOTHER BUDGIE TRICK!
TRINNG!
HE'D RING A BELL!
WELL?
IT WASN'T ME! IT WAS MY BUDGIE! ER, I MEAN...
HOP
HOP
GNEE! GNEE!
SOMETIMES I BET HE GAVE YOU PLAYFUL PECKS!
YOWP!
PECK
VOICE PROFESSOR
PLEASE ENTER
PECK
JUMP
I'VE FOUND MY BUDGIE!
THE RAIN IN SPAIN FALLS MAINLY DOWN A DRAIN.
HOW SWEET!
POSH VOICE
YUCK!
THAT UGLY BIRD NEEDS LESSONS TOO...
WHO'S A PRETTY BOY THEN? — HUH!
RIGHT! LET ME HEAR THAT AGAIN WITHOUT THE 'HUH'!

A SMALL PROBLEM
WHEN I WAS VERY YOUNG I WAS TINY . . .
GRRR!
RASP!
GNBAH! CAN'T REACH!
SWISH!
GNNNG! THESE'LL HELP.
DOG FOOD
I'LL BE TALL ENOUGH NOW!
ONLY ONE PROBLEM . . .
. . . THE CAT HAS MOVED AGAIN.
NEVER MIND . . .
JUMP
. . . I'LL HANG ON TO THESE!
GRAB
GNEE-HEE!
SQUASH!
MEOW YOWP!
But—
OH-OH! HE'S GOING UP A TREE.
LUCKY I'M NOT THE ONLY THING ROUND HERE THAT HASN'T GROWN YET.
PLUCK
. . . THE TREE'S PRETTY SMALL TOO.

DENNIS' WEATHER REPORT
THERE'S FOG APPROACHING!
IGNORE THE RUFFIANS NEXT DOOR, CHUMS!
YES! LET'S GET ON WITH OUR TEDDY BEAR'S PICNIC.
HAW-HAW!
SLOBBER! I WANNA STEAK!
WHIRR!
SPLUTTER!
FUNNY! IT'S ONLY FOGGY IN WALTER'S GARDEN. HO-HO!
GLOOP!
EEKUMS!

WATER WAY TO ACT!
WHAT'S THAT?
SOFT SKIP!
GENTLE TRAMP!
GNEH?
SOFTY—IT'S NOT GOING TO RAIN TODAY—YOU DON'T NEED WELLIES!
TRAMP! TRAMP! TRAMP!
I'M GOING TO TIDY UP THE OLD CANAL. IT'S AN EYESORE!
HMM! HOW DO I GET DOWN THERE?
GNASH!
HAR! HAR! GNASHER'S GLAD TO BE OF SERVICE, WALTER!
SPLUDGE!
I'LL START OFF BY CLEARING THIS HORRIBLE THING AWAY!
HUH! IT'S NOT BOTHERING ANYONE!
EEK! A CANAL MONSTER!
HAW! HAW! RASHER WAS HAVING HIS MORNING WALLOW!
GNEE! GNEE!
WAH!
OINK! OINK!

Soon—
GROAN!
TUM-TE-TUM!
QUICK GROWING SEED
POUR
TUG
HOW SOFT CAN YOU GET?
EEAGH!
...AND THE FINAL TOUCH!
RECOIL
POUR
PERFUME
NICE PONG
AROMA
LOVELY NIFF
SUCH AN IMPROVEMENT!
HUH! IT LOOKED FAR MORE MENACING THE OLD WAY!
WHO'S THAT?
SOB!
SOB!
SOB! THERE'S NO PLACE FOR US HERE ANYMORE!
SOB!
WATER RATS
I KNOW JUST THE PLACE.
I'VE MADE THE NEIGHBOURHOOD A MORE BEAUTIFUL PLACE!
But—
GASP!
SWOON
GRAB
GASP! THOSE HORRORS FROM THE CANAL — IN MY GARDEN!
HEH! I'M SURE YOU'LL ALL BE VERY HAPPY! AHEM!
WALTER'S HOUSE
LOVELY!
STEAM
SHAKE
OINK! SNURFLE!

G'DAY, COBBERS!
At 4P.M.
JUMP
HI, GNASHER—SCHOOL HASN'T BEEN TOO AWFUL TODAY—WALTER THE SOFTY WAS OFF!
SNIFFLE! I HAD TO STAY OFF SCHOOL TODAY—I HAD A WHOLE SNEEZE LAST NIGHT!
HMMM...
WOW! THEN YOU WON'T KNOW WHAT SPECIAL THING WE'RE DOING AT SCHOOL TOMORROW!
MAKING THIS UP
GOSH, NO! HARD SUMS? LONG ESSAYS? WHAT?
NONE OF THAT BORING STUFF. WE'RE HAVING A ROLF HARRIS PARTY!
OH, THAT AUSTRALIAN CHAPPIE ON CHILDREN'S TV!
WE'D BETTER GET YOU READY—EVERYONE ELSE WILL BE DRESSED LIKE ROLF TOMORROW...
TUG
OH, DEAR!
THERE!
DAB DAB
PAINT
HMM. NOT MUCH CHANCE OF YOU GROWING A BEARD IN TIME...
OOER!
RUB

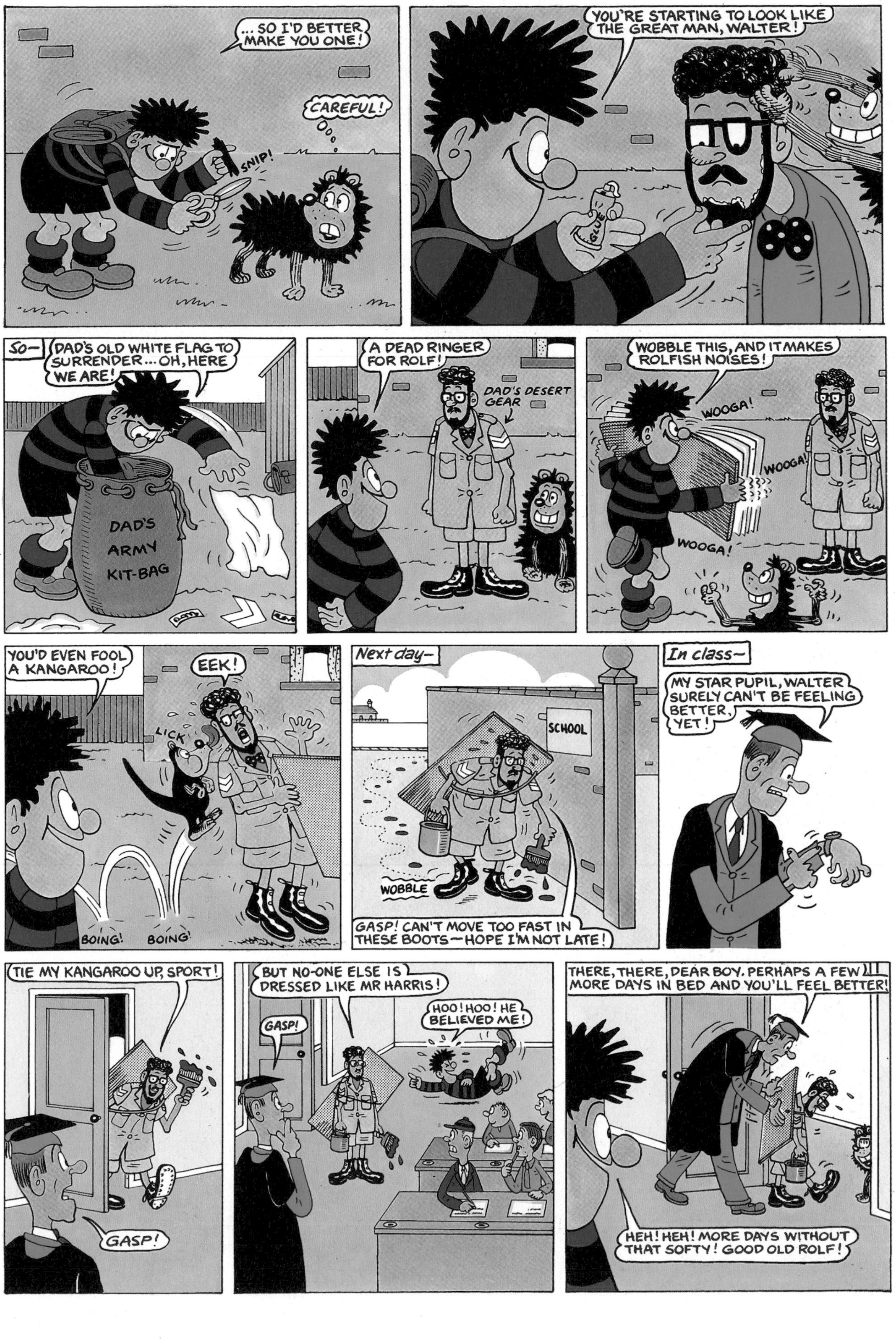

... SO I'D BETTER MAKE YOU ONE!
CAREFUL!
SNIP!
YOU'RE STARTING TO LOOK LIKE THE GREAT MAN, WALTER!
GLUE
SO—
DAD'S OLD WHITE FLAG TO SURRENDER... OH, HERE WE ARE!
DAD'S ARMY KIT-BAG
A DEAD RINGER FOR ROLF!
DAD'S DESERT GEAR
WOBBLE THIS, AND IT MAKES ROLFISH NOISES!
WOOGA!
WOOGA!
WOOGA!
YOU'D EVEN FOOL A KANGAROO!
EEK!
LICK
BOING!
BOING!
Next day—
SCHOOL
WOBBLE
GASP! CAN'T MOVE TOO FAST IN THESE BOOTS—HOPE I'M NOT LATE!
In class—
MY STAR PUPIL, WALTER SURELY CAN'T BE FEELING BETTER, YET!
TIE MY KANGAROO UP, SPORT!
GASP!
BUT NO-ONE ELSE IS DRESSED LIKE MR HARRIS!
GASP!
HOO! HOO! HE BELIEVED ME!
THERE, THERE, DEAR BOY. PERHAPS A FEW MORE DAYS IN BED AND YOU'LL FEEL BETTER!
HEH! HEH! MORE DAYS WITHOUT THAT SOFTY! GOOD OLD ROLF!

DESPERATELY SEEKING SOFTIES
GNASHER'S THE WORLD'S GREATEST SOFTY-SEEKING MISSILE.
ONCE HE'S HOMED IN ON THE SMELL OF A SOFTY...
SNIFF!
... NOTHING CAN STOP HIM. HE'S LIKE A GUIDED MISSILE!
SNIFF!
ZOOM!
EEK! GNASHER! WHERE CAN I HIDE? AHA...
SOFTY WALTER
SNIFF!
PERFUME FACTORY
LOVELY PERFUME NIFF
THIS SHOULD CONFUSE THAT BEASTLY DOG!
EAU DE LOVELY
COME IN AND HAVE A NIFF
ADORABLE AROMA
LOVELY SMELL
SWEET FRAGRANT SMELL
TOO MANY SOFT SMELLS IN HERE— GNASHER CAN'T PICK OUT WALTER!
SILENT MIRTH

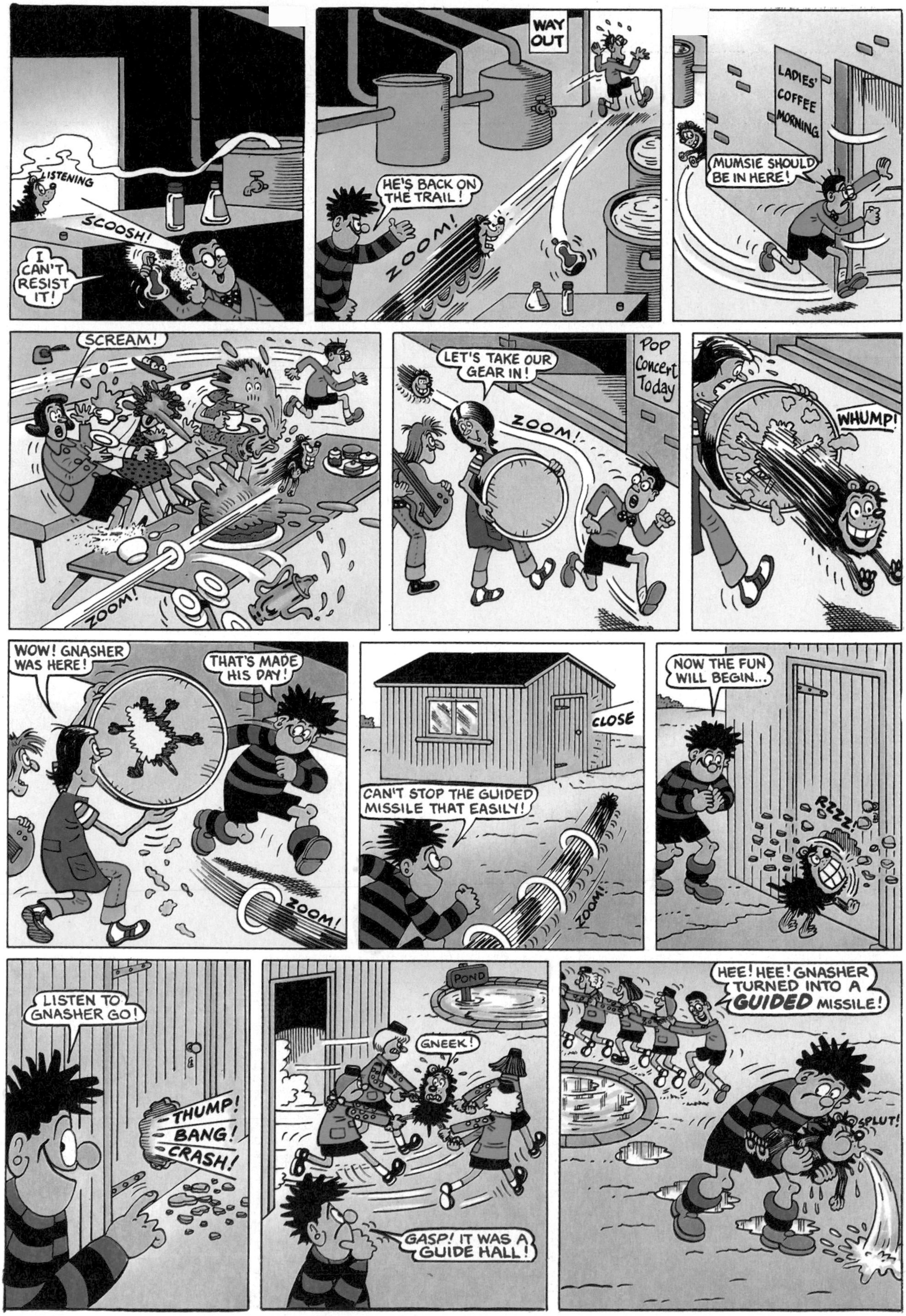
LISTENING
SCOOSH!
I CAN'T RESIST IT!
WAY OUT
HE'S BACK ON THE TRAIL!
ZOOM!
LADIES' COFFEE MORNING
MUMSIE SHOULD BE IN HERE!
SCREAM!
ZOOM!
Pop Concert Today
LET'S TAKE OUR GEAR IN!
ZOOM!
WHUMP!
WOW! GNASHER WAS HERE!
THAT'S MADE HIS DAY!
ZOOM!
CLOSE
CAN'T STOP THE GUIDED MISSILE THAT EASILY!
ZOOM!
NOW THE FUN WILL BEGIN...
RZZZ!
LISTEN TO GNASHER GO!
THUMP!
BANG!
CRASH!
POND
GNEEK!
GASP! IT WAS A GUIDE HALL!
HEE! HEE! GNASHER TURNED INTO A GUIDED MISSILE!
SPLUT!

HAPPY
BIRTHDAY,
PIE-FACE
WHAT DID YOU GET FOR YOUR BIRTHDAY, PIE-FACE?
I GOT THIS SPECIAL GAME OF DRAUGHTS!
HMPH!
I WIN!

CHOMP!
GAME OVER! CHOMP!
MUNCH!
GUZZLE!
I GOT THIS BIG, BASS DRUM . . .
. . . WITH PIES INSIDE!
MUNCH!
BOOM! BOOM!
MARCH!
THEN THERE'S THIS HAT MY UNCLE FROM AUSTRALIA SENT!
TO- PIE-FACE
FROM- OZ
THIS WAY UP!
GREAT PRESENT!
CHOMP!
MUNCH!
HE SURE LIKES PIES!
PIE-FACE

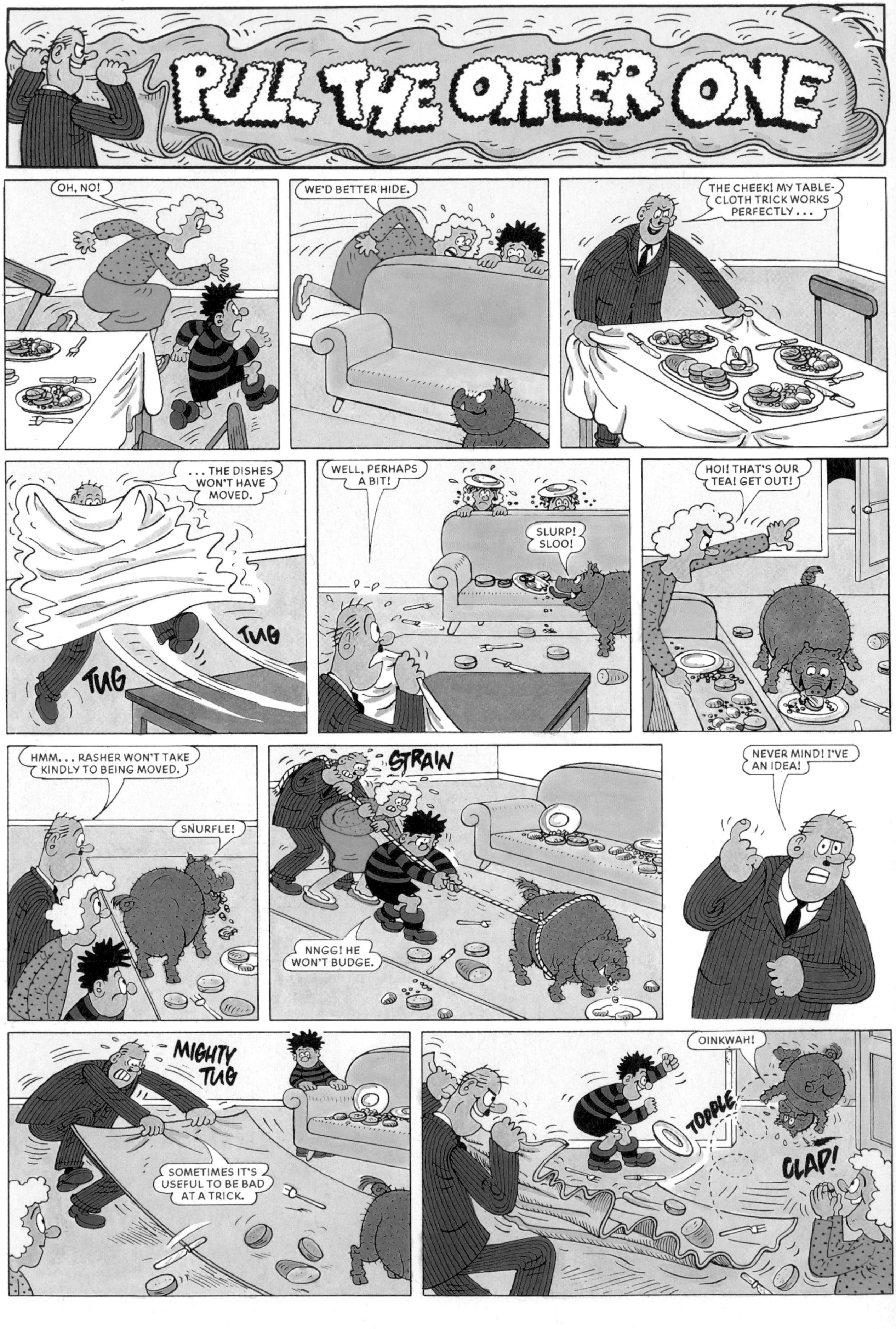
PULL THE OTHER ONE
OH, NO!
WE'D BETTER HIDE.
THE CHEEK! MY TABLE-CLOTH TRICK WORKS PERFECTLY . . .
. . . THE DISHES WON'T HAVE MOVED.
TUG
TUG
WELL, PERHAPS A BIT!
SLURP! SLOO!
HOI! THAT'S OUR TEA! GET OUT!
HMM. . . RASHER WON'T TAKE KINDLY TO BEING MOVED.
SNURFLE!
STRAIN
NNGG! HE WON'T BUDGE.
NEVER MIND! I'VE AN IDEA!
MIGHTY TUG
SOMETIMES IT'S USEFUL TO BE BAD AT A TRICK.
OINKWAH!
TOPPLE
CLAP!

DENNIS' WEATHER REPORT
HAILSTONES SOON!
FILL YOUR GOBS, PALS!
SPECIAL OFFER! GOBSTOPPERS
Boutique
PTOO-PTOO-PTOO!
HAILSTONES? IN JULY?
OOYAH! PAINFUL!

SIMPLY THE NEST!
WE MUST PROVIDE SUITABLE NESTING MATERIAL FOR THE BIRDIES. IT'S NEST BUILDING TIME.
HMM.
TWEET! TWEET!
HOW DO YOU SPELL 'TO'?
WONDER WHAT THAT SIGN SAYS?
Nest site to Let
AH! NICE AND WARM!
IT'S WORKING!
Nest site to Let
OH, DEAR— DON'T WANT TO DISTURB THE NICE BIRDIE!
BET THE BIRD WOULD LIKE SOMETHING TO EAT.
WEAVE
NICE, TASTY WORM, BIRDIE!
CHEEP! SLURP!
SNAP SHUT
PLOP!
SCREAM!
GNEE! GNEE!
OOPS! BUTTER FINGERS!

LET'S HELP WALTER AND GET THE COSIEST NEST AROUND, FOR THE BIRDS.
SO—
WALTER'S ROOM
WALTER'S FANCY BED WILL MAKE A SUPER NEST FOR A BIG BIRD.
PUSH
WALTER'S HOUSE
UP SHE GOES!
TUG
PUSH
THERE—A FINE NEST FOR ANY BIRD!
RUB
CREAK!
CREAK!
GET MY BED DOWN!
THINK THE TREE HEARD YOU, WALTER!
TWANG!
KWATCH THIS NEST
CRACK!
YOWL!
GET THIS BED OFF ME!
TSK, TSK, NO BIRD WILL NEST THERE WITH THAT NOISE GOING ON, WALTER!
SOON—
HUNGRY WORK MENACING —NOW FOR MY OWN DINNER.
GNASHER
WHAT HAVE YOU GOT FOR A GROWING MENACE, MUM?
YUGH! BIRD'S NEST SOUP!
IT CAME FLYING THROUGH THE WINDOW AND LANDED IN YOUR PLATE, DENNIS!
TITTER!
SERVES THAT 'NESTY' BOY RIGHT!

TAKE A RUN AND JUMP
ARE YOU READY, GNASHER?
GNESH!
YIPPEE!
GNASHOO!
ERK?
EEK!
LEAP
ZOOM!
DENNIS! WHAT'S GOING ON?
BOING!
POING!
IT'S OUR 24 HOUR SPONSORED RUN AND JUMP, DAD. WE'VE BEEN SPONSORED TO RUN AND JUMP NON-STOP FOR A WHOLE DAY!
DON'T BE DAFT, GNASHER, DOGS CAN'T CLIMB TREES!
TOLD YOU!
CRUMP!
GROO!

DENNIS! STOP THIS NONSENSE!
CAN'T, DAD! WE'VE BEEN SPONSORED!
GRRR! SPONSORED OR NOT, I'M PUTTING A STOP TO THIS!
ERK!
WHOOPS! THINK I MISJUDGED THAT ONE!
ZZIIIP!
CRASH!
THAT'S THE END! NO MORE OF THIS NONSENSE!
SORRY, DAD, GOT TO KEEP IT UP!
YOU CAN'T VERY WELL STOP THEM IF PEOPLE HAVE SPONSORED THEM TO DO IT, DEAR!
ZOOM!
THERE IS ONE WAY TO STOP US, DAD!
ZOOM!
ZOOM!
YOU COULD TAKE OVER THE SPONSORSHIP SO OTHERS DON'T HAVE TO PAY!
EEK!
ZOOM!
ZOOM!
YES! THEN THEY COULD STOP RUNNING AND JUMPING!
VERY WELL, NO DOUBT IT WILL BE WORTH IT. HOW MUCH HAVE YOU BEEN SPONSORED FOR?
FIVE POUNDS!
WHO EXACTLY SPONSORED THEM ANYWAY—AND WHY?
WAAAH! HE'S FOOLED ME AGAIN!
HAR! HAR! TO MAKE UP FOR STOPPED POCKET MONEY!
Dennis and Gnasher sponsor themselves for £5
GNEE! GNEE!
GURRR!
COME ON, GNASHER! WE'D BETTER KEEP ON RUNNING AND JUMPING FOR A BIT LONGER!

WET VET!
KEEP OFF THE GRASS
GNERK!
THROB
I WANT TO BE A VET WHEN I'M BIG, AND MAKE THINGS WELL.
UGH! YOU MAKE ME SICK!
WALTER, SOFTER THAN WARM BUTTER
A MENACE DOG WON'T WEAR A SOFT BANDAGE!
SNIP!
TOLD YOU—IT WON'T LAST A MINUTE!
OH DEAR —AHA!
GNASH! BITE!
THIS IS A GOOD VET'S TRICK!
PLASTIC BUCKET
CUT
HMM...
PLOP!
HEE! HEE! IT WORKED!
CLAP!
GNASH! GNASH!

WHAT AN UNUSUAL LITTER BIN!
PLOP!
GET IT OFF QUICK, WALTER—OR THERE'S GOING TO BE SOME SOFTY GNASHING!
GNASHUMPH!
ER—WE'LL TRY SOMETHING ELSE!
TUG
PYOINNG!
FISH—YUCK!
SPREAD
FISH PASTE
HERE COME THE CATS!
YUM!
PONG!
FISHY
SMELL
PONG!
GNASH! GNASH! GNASH! GNASH!
THERE GO THE CATS!
CHOMPRIP!
HAD ENOUGH
YOU'RE BEING A SILLY DOG—YOUR SORE PAW WON'T GET BETTER!
WAIT TILL YOU SEE WHAT'S WRONG WITH HIM!
THIS IS WHAT IS BOTHERING MY TOUGH DOG!
OOH! LOOKS LIKE A FLOWER STUCK IN HIS PAW!
OO-ER! I WAS WRONG CALLING HIM A SILLY DOG, WASN'T I?
YOU WANTED TO BE A VET AND BANDAGE UP ANIMALS, EH?
WHOOSHGNASHYOWL
GLOOMFF!
SO GNASHER'S DECIDED TO BE A DOCTOR AND BANDAGE UP SOFTIES! HAR! HAR!
ICE
DUST

WALTER'S jolly super inventions for Softies!
THE TIDYTOES TOENAIL CLIPPERS
SAVES ALL THAT TIRESOME BENDING!
SNIP!
SO COSY ON THE TUM ON COLD DAYS!
HOT WATER TUMMY BELT
IT KEEPS MY PRECIOUS TEDDY SNUG AND COMFY!
PAPOOSE CARRIER FOR TEDDIES
IT MAKES SURE YOUR FOOTWEAR DAZZLES ALL DAY LONG!
SHINYSHOE ELECTRIC POLISHER
WHIRR! POLISH!
I'D LIKE ALL THAT STUFF WALTER!
Y-Y-YOU W-WOULD?

SNIP!
HANDY FOR FRUIT PICKING!
YOWL!
SPLAT!
GLUB!
BETTER THAN A WATER PISTOL!
WALLOP!
THE TEDDY CARRIER MAKES A PERFECT CATAPULT!
POND
PYOING!
SQUEAL! POOR TEDDY!
GLUMPH!
ANOTHER GREAT MENACE DEVICE!
WHIRR!
POLISH!

M-M-MENACE
NOT EVERYONE'S GOT A STRIPED JERSEY LIKE MINE OR SPIKEY HAIR, SO I'M GOING TO SHOW YOU HOW TO LET PEOPLE KNOW YOU'RE A MENACE!
THE DREADED "M" FOR MENACE SIGN.
MAKE THE "M" FOR MENACE SIGN AND EVERYONE WILL KNOW YOU'RE A MENACE!
SLAM!
SLAM!
SLAM!
SLAM!
SLAM!
TUM-TEE-TUM— HOW LOVELY!
FAIRY SANDCASTLE
SOFTY WALTER
Then—
EEK! THE SIGN OF THE MENACE!
DIVE
H-HELP!
SEE THE EFFECT IT HAS ON SOFTIES, READERS!

BOXING CLUB
WE DON'T THINK YOU'RE SO TOUGH!
"M" FOR MENACE TIME AGAIN!
WHAT'S THIS?
NOT SO TOUGH, EH?
SWING
ZOOM!
OOYAH!
EEAGH!
CRUMP!
CRUMP!
"M" FOR MENACE AGAIN!
HELLO, FELLOW MENACES!
DENNIS'S GRAN
SWOON
HEH! HEH! IT'S CATCHING ON. ANYONE CAN DO IT!
ANYONE?
HEH! HEH! GNASHER'S MAKING THE "M" SIGN!
TOPPLE
DOGNEEK!
THUD!
CRUMP!
THE ONLY MENACES WHO SHOULDN'T TRY IT...
... ARE MENACING DOGS, HEH! HEH!
GNASH! GNASH!

WHEN I WAS YOUR AGE...
AW, GRANNY! OLDEN DAYS WERE RUBBISH!
...CLOTHES!
NOW...
CHANGING ROOM
BHS
Changing Room
Then
Bathing Costume
7/6
...SCHOOL!
NOW...
TAP!
TAP!
TAP!
ALIEN DEATH WOTSIT
TAP!
TAP! TAP!
SCRAPE!
SKREEK!
cat
Then
...FOOTBALL!
NOW...
Ryan Giggs
Alec James
Then...

...CINEMA!
Vooo
POPCORN
Then...
SOAP
...FOOD!
Wooo
Mega Cola
Then...
BEST TRIPE
SCHLOPP!
...WARFARE!
Wooo
FLOUR
POWDERED EGG
COD LIVER OIL
BRYL CREEM
WALTER'S GRANDMAMA
GNASHER'S GRANFER
Then...
WOW! I WAS WRONG! OLDEN DAYS WERE FAB!
YEE-HEE-HEE! SOME THINGS NEVER CHANGE!

WHO'S COMPLAINING?
BILL
BILL
DONK!
WAHEY!
BARBER
GNASH! GNASH!
EEK!
Six o'clock—
I'M JUST HOME FROM WORK— NOW TO START MY REAL WORK!
KNOCK!
KNOCK!
IT'S THE DAILY COMPLAINTS QUEUE!
COMPLAIN, COMPLAIN!
MOAN! GRUMBLE!
BILL
BILL
THIS ISN'T THE FIRST TIME THIS HAS HAPPENED, READERS...
BILL
BILL
SUPPLIERS TO THE DENNIS QUEUE
Hot Tea
HOT SNACKS
SUPPLIERS TO THE DENNIS COMPLAINTS QUEUE
IN FACT THESE VANS DO RECORD BUSINESS...
... AND THEY'VE HAD TO BUILD THIS CAR PARK FOR ALL THE CARS!
CAR PARK for DENNIS QUEUERS ONLY
MUST SEE DENNIS'S DAD!

DENNIS BROKE MY WINDOW!
BILL
GROAN!
BILL
HOLD IT A MOMENT, FOLKS!
DOCTOR PROCTOR
FRUIT PIES
SORE EARS
AH!
THERE, OLD CHAP—YOU SHOULD BE ABLE TO CARRY ON NOW!
SOOTHING LOTION
BILL
Then—
LET ME GUESS—HE WATER PISTOLLED YOU, HE PUT A FROG IN YOUR SOUP, AND NAILED YOUR SHOES TO THE FLOOR...
NO...
BILL
...DENNIS HAS NEVER MENACED ME! I FEEL TOTALLY LEFT OUT!
GASP!
PLEASE GET HIM TO MENACE ME, SO I CAN FEEL NORMAL. PLEASE!
DENNIS—MENACE THIS MAN!
EH? OK!
TA!
SNATCH
CONSIDER YOURSELF MENACED!
SPLAT!
HAPPY NOW?
BILL
NO! I'D LIKE TO COMPLAIN ABOUT YOUR SON MENACING ME!
IT TAKES ALL KINDS TO FORM THE MENACE QUEUE!
B-BUT...

THE AGE OLD QUESTION
I KNOW LOTS OF 'BEANO' FACTS...
NOEL THE KNOW-ALL
BUT I DON'T KNOW HOW OLD DENNIS IS. SCREAM!
R-I-P!
READERS
WE WANT TO KNOW TOO!
LATER
I'M DOING AN AGE CENSUS. HOW OLD ARE YOU, SON?
I'LL TELL YOU...
GASP! HE'S TRICKED DENNIS!
COUNT THE SPINS AND YOU'LL KNOW HOW OLD I AM!
SPIN
SPIN
I L-LOST C-COUNT!
NO-ONE GETS TO KNOW THE MENACE'S AGE!
STAGGER
GNEE GNEE!
SPIN

THWACK!
YOU CAN TELL A TREE'S AGE FROM ITS RINGS...
MAYBE YOU CAN TELL A MENACE'S AGE BY THE AMOUNT OF BIG SPIKES HE HAS IN HIS HAIR!
...THREE, FOUR...
YEEOW!
SNAP!
IT WASN'T MY HAIR- IT WAS GNASHER!
LET'S GET SOME CREAM FOR YOUR GNASHED FINGER!
HAR! HAR! HE'LL NEVER FIND OUT MY AGE!
STAMP!
IF ONLY I KNEW WHEN THESE WERE TAKEN!
WHAT'S THIS?
FLOP
IT'S DENNIS'S BIRTH CERTIFICATE. I KNOW HOW OLD HE IS – I'M GOING TO SHOW THE READERS!
ZOOM!
QUICK, GNASHER!
ZOOM!
ZOOM!
WHO AM I? WHERE AM I? WHAT HAPPENED?
HE'S FORGOTTEN EVERYTHING!
PHEWWW!
WAAH, MY SECRET!
GNERK!
IF YOU FIND DENNIS'S BIRTH CERTIFICATE READERS – DON'T LOOK AT IT, OK?
– EDITOR'S NOTE.

GIVE IT SOME ELBOW!
REMEMBER I SHOWED YOU THIS A FEW PAGES AGO...
THE "M" FOR MENACE SIGN
...AND IMPORTANT PARTS OF MY "M" FOR MENACE SIGN...
ROLL
...ARE KNOBBLY ELBOWS!
TRING!
BRING!
BRRING!
DRING!
WHAT DO YOU WANT?
GRR! WHAT DO YOU WANT?
WHO RANG MY BELL?
WASN'T ME!
A GREAT FEATURE OF A MENACE, THESE ARE!
GNESH! GNESH!

AHA!
WALTER PRINCE OF SOFTIES
MAY I JOIN IN?
IF YOU'RE NOT ROUGH!
THUMP!
WAIL!
THUD!
NEVER MIND, HAVE SOME POP!
SPLODGE!
THEY'RE LOOKING WELL TODAY, MENACES!
SWISH!
KARATE EXPERT
HMMM!
OUT OF THE WAY, YOU!
JAB
THROB
THE ELBOW FAILED!
THUMP!
NO, IT DIDN'T, GNASHER!
BLOW
TOPPLE
LATER
YOU'VE HEARD OF TENNIS ELBOW, READERS...
...WELL I'VE GOT MENACE ELBOW! GROAN.
AND A GOOD THING TOO!
ELBOW LOTION
ELBOW LOTION

DENNIS' WEATHER REPORT
SNOW NEXT.
IT'S SIMPLY SOOPER!
HI, DENNIS. DO YOU WANT A SPIFFING HAIRDO, TOO?
ME?
NO-NO-NO-NO-NO-NO-NO-NO-!
AARGH! A DANDRUFF BLIZZARD!
GNO-GNO!

RECORD BREAKERS
ONE PEACEFUL DAY . . .
CLICK!
CLICK!
Z-Z-Z
PLOP!
KNIT
STOP IT! I WON'T LET YOU PLAY THAT NOISY STUFF ON MY RECORD PLAYER.
So—
STICK YOUR CLAW THROUGH THIS HOLE, GNASHER.
PLOP!
THEN I'LL GIVE IT A SPIN.
SPIN
PUT DOWN YOUR OTHER CLAW . . .
PUSH
SCRAPE
. . . AND I'VE GOT A RECORD PLAYER. NOT VERY LOUD, THOUGH.
SCRAPE
SPIN
SO I'LL ROLL UP MUM'S MAG.
ROLL
PERFECT!
NOT TOO IMPRESSED
THIS IS AWFUL!
AH! AT LEAST GNASHER DOES SOMETHING MY RECORD PLAYER DOESN'T . . .
WAH!
CRUNCH!
CRUNCH!
. . . HE GETS RID OF BAD RECORDS.

CUFF LINK
I CAN NEVER GET SOFT WALTER TO COME MENACING WITH ME.
TWIRL
So—
SHAKE HANDS, WALTER!
OOH! DENNIS WANTS TO LIVE IN PEACE WITH ME!
But—
EEK!
CLICK!
NOW YOU'VE GOT TO COME MENACING WITH ME, WALTER!
OH, HORRORS!
TUG
WH-WHAT ARE YOU GOING TO DO?
DRAG
SOFTY SLAP!
GURRR!
EEK! WE SHOULDN'T HAVE DONE THAT, DENNIS!
WE? I DIDN'T TOUCH HIM!

EEK!
SCREAM!
OOYAH!
HE TIED MY NOSE IN A KNOT. THAT WAS YOUR FAULT, DENNIS!
COME ON, LET'S DO A MENACING DARE!
DRAG
OVER WE GO!
TUG
MUDDY BOG
SPLUDGE!
OOPS! FORGOT THERE WASN'T ENOUGH ROOM FOR BOTH OF US!
In the park—
OH, DEAR— IT'S TOO BUSY...
DAZED
EEK!
WHIRL
SPIN
NEVER MIND—WE CAN HAVE OUR OWN ROUNDABOUT!
HMMM —THAT ROUNDABOUT WAS A LITTLE TOO FAST FOR YOU!
DIZZY
BED TIME, DENNIS!
BED TIME, WALTER!
OH, NO! I'VE LOST MY KEY...
...WORST THING ABOUT THESE HANDCUFFS...
In Walter's bedroom—
...WE CAN'T BE SEPARATED TILL WE GET A NEW KEY TOMORROW! THE SHAME!

STONE ME
WALTER, HEAD WIMP
FOO-FOO
WHAT SOFTIE NONSENSE IS THIS?
MY PRECIOUS POODLE DESERVES A PRECIOUS STONE IN HIS COLLAR!
SORRY I CAN'T BUY YOU ONE, PAL— MY POCKET MONEY'S STOPPED FOR 50 YEARS!
I'VE A PRECIOUS STONE...
DRAG
...A MENACE STONE!
POO! POO! THAT'S WORTHLESS!
HERE'S WHY IT'S SO PRECIOUS!
TWANG!
YOU CAN'T LOSE IT!
BONK!

QUACK! QUACK!
GNERK! THE STONE WILL SINK!
YEEK!
SKIP
SKIP
SQUEAL!
TOPPLE
SPLASH!
BOO-HOO!
GREAT MENACING STONE!
SWISH!
UNBEATABLE CONKER, THIS IS!
SWISH!
UNBEATABLE, EH?
SWISH!
ULP!
SHATTER!
SLIP OUT
IT'LL BE SMASHED!
BRRRM!
THE DRILL, THAT IS!
JEWELLER
SHATTER!
BOO-HOO!
GASP! THIS IS A VERY RARE MENACIUM STONE! HARDER THAN DIAMOND! I'LL GIVE YOU ANYTHING FOR IT!
ANYTHING?
Later—
READER
WHY ARE YOU WEARING SUN GLASSES, WALTER?
HAR-HAR! SO MY MENACE STONE WASN'T PRECIOUS, EH?
I'M BLINDED!
DAZZLE
DAZZLE

BARMY ARMY
WAH! IS IT A MAD BULL?
SNORT!
NO! I'M IN A BAD MOOD!
SNORT!
WE'RE GOING ON A SCHOOL TRIP TODAY — I HATE THEM!
SCHOOL BUS
ARE WE GOING TO VISIT A FLOWER DISPLAY, TEACHER?
NO, WE'VE COME TO SEE THE SPECIAL 'VERY TOUGH SQUAD' IN ACTION!
OOH! HOW TOUGH!
SAPS!
WHAT DID YOU SAY?
VTS
ARE YOU DEAF? — I SAID YOU WERE SAPS!
EEK!
TWEAK
VTS

I MEAN, ANYONE CAN DO THIS!
GNESH!
PUSH
RUMBLE!
EVERYONE EXCEPT YOU LOT!
THUD!
THUD!
THUD!
HELP! MUMMY!
FLATTEN
RASP!
COME BACK, MENACE!
PUSH
BUMP
NO- YOU GO BACK!
BOOMFF!
BUMP!
BUMP!
BUMP!
HE'LL HELP ME TO GET RID OF THE REST OF THESE SOLDIERS!
GENERAL
Soon-
GENERAL IN HIS UNDERWEAR
GO OUT INTO THE COUNTRY AND MESS ABOUT FOR A WHILE!
YES, SIR!
YES, GENERAL!
PAH!
THE NAUGHTY BOY!
I MUST DO SOME MORE MENACING!
BANG!
BANG!
STUCK
WE'VE GOT HIM!
BAH! BEATEN BY A SOFTY AFTER ALL THAT!
OUR HERO!

HIPPY SHAKER
I WONDER WHAT MY BACK LEGS LOOK LIKE — MY STOMACH'S STOPPED ME SEEING THEM FOR A WHILE.
RASHER WILL HAVE TO LOSE WEIGHT.
TRY SOME YOGA TO MAKE YOU SLIM.
YOGA
WELL, I'VE MANAGED TO BEND MY LEGS . . .
COIL
COIL
. . . BUT THEY'RE A BIT SPRINGY.
UNCOIL
SPRING
WAH! I THOUGHT I SAW A FLYING PIG — MUST SEE MY PSYCHIATRIST.
BEST PRICES FOR OLD CLOTHES
WOW! AN EASTERN GURU. I CAN TELL BY THE STOMACH.
GROO!
HIPPY
TELL US SOME WISDOM, O FAT GURU!
SNURK!
SNURK, MAN! IT'S THE MAGIC WORD.
SNURK!
SNURK!
SNURK? THAT'S PIG TALK!
HE'S NO GURU — HE'S A PIG!
THESE PEOPLE WEREN'T TOO HAPPY . . .
. . . BUT THEY HELPED WITH MY YOGA.
TIED
SNURK! YURK!

THE BEANO
DENNIS the MENACE and
ZONK
RUB
THAT'S ALL FOR NOW - BUT YOU CAN FIND DENNIS AND GNASHER IN THE BEANO OUT EVERY WEDNESDAY.